**Mel Bay Presents Stefan Grossman's Guitar Workshop Audio Series**

# Larry Coryell
## Jazz Guitar

### Exercises, Scales, Modes & Techniques

*taught by Larry Coryell*

1 2 3 4 5 6 7 8 9 0

*Visit us on the Web at www.melbay.com — E-mail us at email@melbay.com*

# One-On-One with Larry Coryell

## by Dr. Joe Barth

Born April 2, 1943 in Galveston, Texas, Larry Coryell played piano as a child, then as a teenager, switched to the guitar. He went on to carve out his unique voice as a jazz fusion guitarist in the late '60's and '70's. Early on he played with Chico Hamilton, Gary Burton and Herbie Mann and has gone on to play with many other great jazz musicians of our time. I caught up with Larry when he was in Pittsburgh, PA, preparing for a performance with an ensemble that included Benny Golson, Wallace Roney, John Patitucci and others.

**JB:** *Larry, did you come from a musical family?*
**LC:** Yes, and no. My mother played some piano and she sang and encouraged me to be musical and to sing. My birth father I actually never knew. I believe he died rather early on. But not much more is known about him except that he was a pianist. He played jazz piano and sang, and that's all I know.

**JB:** *What was your first guitar?*
**LC:** I'm not sure. It might have been a very cheap round-holed acoustic that came out of a Sears-Roebuck or a Montgomery Ward catalog.

**JB:** *Were there any local players that inspired you?*
**LC:** Yeah. After my family moved to Richland, Washington, there was a local fellow, a great jazz guitarist named John LaChapelle. I studied with him for a while.

**JB:** *Were there any other guitar teachers you worked with?*
**LC:** Yes, I worked with a guy that taught Chet Atkins style. We were way out there in the boondocks and country-western music was quite prevalent. His name was Danny Love. His day gig was wheat inspection but he also taught guitar at the same music store in Richland, Washington that John LaChapelle taught at.

**JB:** *Did you study music at the University of Washington?*
**LC:** The only music courses I took were music courses for non-majors. Once, the professor who taught those courses, mentioned that he had heard Charlie Parker, he and I became instant friends. I grilled him about Bird and I learned a lot from him. He was especially good with music appreciation. I believe It was in his class that I first heard *Black, Brown and Beige* by Duke Ellington, and the *Porgy and Bess* album by Miles Davis.

**JB:** *How old were you when you started playing jazz guitar?*
**LC:** I really can't remember. I tried to play jazz when I was about eighteen or nineteen, perhaps a little earlier, but I don't really think I sounded very good

**JB:** *Which guitarists did you listen to growing up?*
**LC:** Well, John LaChapelle, aside from teaching me things that I would ask him to teach me, let me browse through his record collection and borrow records and I borrowed records, so I got to hear Les Paul before his multiple recording days—his multi-tracking days. Then I got a really nice Johnny Smith record called *In a Mellow Mood*. And I got a really nice Barney Kessel, in fact a couple of Barney Kessel records. And I got a killer Tal Farlow record that has *Autumn in New York* on it, with Tal tuning his sixth string down to A.

**JB:** *Earlier today while I was listening to your lecture at the University of Pittsburgh, you mentioned Wes Montgomery. When did you first hear Wes?*
**LC:** It was after all the influences I just mentioned, that I heard Wes Montgomery, and his playing just changed my life. Recently I was listening to some previously unreleased Wes Montgomery stuff. Some of it might have been with Harold Land, some of the stuff might have

been with Jimmy Smith. He would move into the octaves and start soloing with the octaves; just incredible. I'll tell you a great recording: *How Insensitive.* I don't know which record that's on. My wife has a Brazilian compilation of his, and the way Wes plays his octave solo on that song is unbelievable. It's so clean. It's so brilliant, the way he chooses his intervals; absolutely brilliant!

**JB:** *From your perspective now, which are the three most influential jazz guitar albums and why?*
**LC:** So hard to select… Well, you know, for some crazy reason I ended up really digging something called *On View at the Five Spot* by Kenny Burrell, and I would like to say that *Red Norvo with Strings* really has to be up there. It is a fantastic showca    for Tal Farlow. And *The Incredible Jazz Guitar of Wes Montgomery.* Even though Wes said he did not like that record.

**JB:** *Did Wes ever say why?*
**LC:** He just didn't think he played very well on it. He liked the way he played on an album called *Full House*, which was recorded live at a place called Tsubo in Berkeley, CA with Johnny Griffin, and that is a great record.

**JB:** *It is a great record.*
**LC:** That was a fantastic record…but I really loved a Wes Montgomery record called *Movin' Along*, which was just a blowing thing. I just loved his tunes.

**JB:** *Which would be the three most important jazz albums by non-guitarists?*

LC: Let me tell you what I think is a great album. I can't remember what it's called. We were talking about it downstairs. We were talking about John Scofield with Joe Henderson, the tribute to Miles.

JB: *Yeah, I have that record, So Near, So Far.*
LC: That is the greatest example of interaction between guitar and saxophone in the last twenty years.

JB: *Okay, are there any others you would...?*
LC: I didn't hear the whole album that Scofield did with Eddy Harris, but I heard one track on the radio and that was again some of the greatest, greatest, interaction of saxophone and guitar I've heard since Gabor Szabo used to play with Charles Lloyd. And before that, the greatest blend of sax and guitar was Johnny Smith with, Zoot Sims, and other times with Stan Getz, *Stars Fell on Alabama*. I can't remember what album it's on.

JB: *That's Johnny Smith's "Moonlight in Vermont album."*
LC: Whoever the saxophone player is...

JB: *That's Stan Getz.*
LC: That is one of the greatest...when Getz does the double-tonguing at the end of his chorus...that's one of the greatest pieces of music I've ever heard. I never get tired of that. It scares me when I hear it because I hear very few players today playing with that kind of originality.

JB: *Are there any jazz albums maybe without a guitar in the combo that would be...?*
LC: Absolutely. *Miles Davis Europe, 1963*. An incredible record! He did *The Complete Concert 1964* and *Giant Steps*, of course.

JB: *Coltrane?*
LC: And his *Love Supreme*.

JB: *Was jazz always your main interest?*
LC: I liked blues. I liked some pop music. I love certain classical music. I wasn't exposed to much of that. When I moved to the east coast in 1965 I started hearing a lot more classical music and discovered Stravinsky, Ravel, Debussy, Shostakovich, Bartok and Wagner.

JB: *Where do you want to go with the guitar, in terms of future expression of ideas?*
LC: Well, there's more than one place I want to go. I want to continue trying to fine-tune and improve my straight-ahead playing. And I feel that a certain percentage of my new CD that came out in January of 2001 reflects that. Not all of it but some of it...it's realizing where I'm trying to go. Especially the way I play *In a Sentimental Mood*. It's something I can actually listen to without shutting off in disgust. I heard some music there. It's really about making music.

JB: *On your recent CD, what ensemble do you have?*
LC: It's John Hicks on piano, Yoron Israel on drums Santi Debriano on bass, and Don Sickler plays trumpet on two tracks. He's the producer. The other things I'm trying to do is to get my orchestral works performed. I wrote a double concerto for two guitars and orchestra, and I think it's a piece of music that deserves to be played more than once.

JB: *You played that in Italy last year, is that correct?*
LC: Yeah, I did it again in March this year with Al DiMeola. If you listen to the *Concerto De Aranjuez* for the four hundred, fifty-seventh billionth time, one of two things will happen. You'll either get tired of it—as great at is, or it will begin to sound like a guy improvising, so why not just have the guitarist, or guitarists, in front of the orchestra do more improvising in certain sections to make it more contemporary and more alive and

more real? Rather than having it in the so-called legitimate format, everything totally written out, and the player is only the soloist, is just allowed to interpret what is written. That's no fun.

Chick Corea has already done it with Mozart. I think Keith Jarrett might have done it with Bartok, I'm not sure. But, I think that's the direction to go as far as concert halls and orchestras. Orchestras aren't getting enough new stuff to play. That's just my guess.

JB: *Of all the albums you have recorded, which two or three are you most pleased with and would want to be known for? I know you have a lot more music that's still to come, but...*
LC: I really can't answer that. I think that *Spaces* was a good record. I think *The Restful Mind* was a good record. I think that *Twin House* was good. Those are all projects with other guitarists. First with McLaughlin, then with Towner, then with Philip Catherine. But, you know, that requires me to bring in too much ego. I don't want to set my own place in guitar history...it's's uncomfortable to me....

JB: *I'm not so much asking from a standpoint of your place in guitar history, but more in terms of just the albums that you felt good about the finished product...*
LC: I'll tell you a really good record; it was called *Air Dancing*. It was on Jazz Point Records, a company now out of business. It was recorded live in Paris with Buster Williams, Stanley Cowell and Billy Hart, and was one of the best records I ever made.

JB: *That is an outstanding record.*
LC: Oh, you know it?

JB: *I have it. Your playing on the Coltrane tune "Impressions" is just breathtaking!*
LC: Yeah, I think that's really a good record.

JB: *About the Spaces album-- how did you choose to assemble the musicians that performed with you on it?*
LC: Just called them up (laughter). I personally hired McLaughlin myself. Oh, as soon as I heard John, I wanted to do a record with him. I asked Danny Weiss, the producer, to call Miroslav Vitous and Chick Corea, and then he suggested Billy Cobham, and then we were complete and it was fine with me. Those guys were all the top cats in New York.

JB: *At the time that you were recording "Spaces," did you sense some special chemistry happening between you and the other musicians?*
LC: Not on the first day. I was mad at all of them. I was trying to kind of guide the direction that I wanted the music to go in, and all the others were such strong individuals that they just did their own thing. It was hilarious... hilarious!

JB: *How many days did it take you to record it?*
LC: Two days. By the second day we had learned the music a little better, and tried to do some different stuff... and, also, John and I had actually practiced and rehearsed *Rene's Theme* prior to going into the studio, so that was ready to go.

JB: *Of course, that's a great tune.*
LC: I'm very proud of it.

JB: *How did you come about selecting the "Spaces Revisited" musicians? Did you contact all the guys that played on the first album?*
LC: It was the same producer. I asked Danny Weiss, about the project and he suggested Richard Bona, the electric bassist.. I heard him play with Joe Zawinul and he sounded perfect. And then I had been softening up (Billy) Cobham for a tour, and to get the tour off the ground we needed to make a record. I had been wanting to do something with

Bireli Lagrene. I like doing things with other guitar players, and I just really enjoyed his playing. I think he's the best of all.

JB: *Moving on to the music you made with "The Eleventh House," what are some notable memories that you have of your time with those musicians?*
LC: Well, in the first installment of the band, with Randy Brecker, Al Mouzon, Mike Mandel and bass player Danny Trifan, there was a first European tour and it was fantastic. I think it took place in '72, I'm not sure. Then we had a reunion --Al Mouzon on drums, John Lee on bass and Shunzo Ono on trumpet. It was just a quartet. We did a live recording at Birdland on October 16, 1999, and it was streamed on a website called "Global Music Network," (GMN). That was one of the best performances we ever gave. I tried to buy that back from the internet company that recorded it and they said that it wasn't even for sale. I think that's a tragedy. That's just the way the cookie crumbles in the music business.

JB: *Is that material not available?*
LC: Only if you download it off the internet. You win a few and you lose a few, you know. You just have to let the chips fall where they may. No regrets.

JB: *You have recorded with some of the best guitarists of this generation. What do you remember fondly about working with some of them. Tell me about your work with John McLaughlin.*
LC: Well, he had the ability to play very unpredictable sequences of notes, very quickly, very fast, very clean, unbelievable technique. He also had a tremendous ability to play uneven time signatures, and he had a firm grasp of modal playing versus cadence playing, and just an incredible imagination and unbelievable drive. Other than that he was a terrible player. (Laughter)

JB: *Have you had the opportunity to work with him since the "Spaces" album?*
LC: Oh, yeah, we did various things at various times in various places. He never changes. He's got that real love of music.

JB: *Tell me about your work with Philip Catherine?*
LC: I really found a real kindred spirit with him. We had so many of the same influences and we had, at least for a few years, an uncanny ability to play really together as a duet. We were able to know where to go in terms of where the other one was and very often we would arrive in unison passages or harmony passages together. We just had a lot of similarities even though I was American and he was European. He had a tremendous love for the traditional, you know, the really basic jazz guitar style, but because he was European, it was blended in with his European influences, most notably Django.

JB: *What about your work with Emily Remler?*
LC: Well, she was really like a straight-ahead player coming out of Pat Martino and Wes Montgomery style. She had a tremendous time feeling, a tremendous sense of swing and a tremendous, almost unbelievable, poetic ability to improvise. She was just a natural player. There was one time when we were on tour in Germany when we were at a doctor's office and she picked up an electric guitar and plugged it in at this doctor's office and played some stuff by herself that was just fantastic. No pick, just playing with her fingers, and she had an unbelievable sound. She knew how to use the amplifier and always knew where she was, and yet she was able to get lost in the playing. She was pretty amazing. She could really swing. Boy could she swing!

JB: *I want to ask you about Birelli Lagrene who played on the "Spaces Revisited" album.*
LC: Boy, what a player. You hear even more of the Django influence,

even more than Phillip—or maybe differently. And Bireli has just unbelievable technique, unbelievable ability to play whatever he hears in his head. Also, any piece of music he hears, he can play it. He can emulate any style. Another thing is that he had just about the strongest hands of anybody. He worked for years, for many hours a day just playing the electric bass, working out Jaco Pastorius-type ideas. He's a natural musician to the n'th degree. He can play anything; he can do anything. I heard him when he was about twelve years old; he was playing like Django Reinhardt, only more so.

JB: *What about your work with Ralph Towner?*
LC: There's an amazing player. Ralph Towner is kind of like the Chick Corea of the guitar. You don't notice it so much unless you're actually playing with him-- his unbelievable presence as a player. You really feel a lot of positive aggressiveness when he's comping, for example; he really pulls those strings. He's not just a delicate, gentle player, he has a tremendous range of dynamics and emotional spectrum in his playing.

JB: *You worked with Steve Khan as well.*
LC: A great rhythm guitar player, unbelievable. Just a very solid musician, and he plays from the heart. He's like McLaughlin in that he just really loves music, really loves the instrument, and has made it his business to become totally versed in all the different styles.

JB: *I know you made one album with the Great Guitars, with Mundell Lowe, Herb Ellis and Charlie Byrd. Reflect upon that experience. Did you just do the one album with them, or were there others?*
LC: We just did the one album. I just wish we could have played together more before we recorded or did more touring and then recorded, because I saw a lot of tremendous possibilities with them. I also really respect all of those guys' wisdom and experience. You know, I never really listened to that record. I do remember that Charlie and I did a version of *My Funny Valentine* on it. I think that came out pretty nice.

JB: *Yeah, it did. I like the whole album.*
LC: And Mundell Lowe has an unbelievable ability to play anything that comes to his head, having his sixth string tuned down a whole step all the time. It's very hard to do.

JB: *He has it that way all the time?*
LC: Almost all the time. And he has an unbelievable sound. Herb Ellis just reminds me so much of Charlie Christian, what Charlie Christian would have been like today. That "Texas thing" that Herb has, he has a tremendous ability to preserve the essence of music as it was taught to him. I hope he continues to be healthy and continue his work as an artist. He could take a tune that wasn't that great, like "I Want to Be Happy," and really make it...

JB: *Something.*
LC: Yeah, really tear it apart (musically) and make something of it. There is a tremendous joy in his playing.

JB: *Are there any guitarists that I have not mentioned that you...*
LC: Well the big three--Abercrombie, Scofield and Metheny-- are all giants in their own way! But I think Abercrombie is just a hair more creative, in that I have never heard him repeat himself. His music, you know that it is jazz, but are very few clichess.

JB: *Have you recorded with Abercrombie?*
LC: Just the *All Strings Attached* video and disc. But he is much better than that. He just got better and better.

JB: *Was that same video the only time you recorded with Scofield?*
LC: Scofield recorded with me on a album called *Tributaries* that I recorded with Joe Beck.

JB: *Did you ever record with Pat Metheny?*
LC: No.

JB: *What non guitarist do you most fondly remember recording with?*
LC: Mirolav Vitous is a fantastic bass player, just fantastic. I did one record date with Kenny Barron. I thought that he was a giant, I was really impressed. I could not believe how he understands how to play bebop. We recorded *Yesterday*. It was the first tune of the session and we ended up doing three takes, maybe because I wasn't happy with my solo, but we could have used any one of his takes; they were all great. He really understood. You know *Yesterday* has a lot of moving circle of fifths, A7 to D7 to G7, he would start with a Bb jazz minor scale on the A7 and go a Eb jazz minor scale for the D7, and so on and so forth. In starting these phrases a 1/2 step above the root of the chord, my mind was split, because I was hearing where the root was and I was hearing where he would start these phrases. Truly, he was playing extended harmony with unbelievable grace. Also there is a saxophonist, Donald Harrison, who has tremendous heart when he plays. He plays with tremendous joy and incredible technique.

JB: *You mentioned Miroslav Vitous.*
LC: He is a genius. He is more than a bassist. He is a composer, orchestrator, and musicologist. There is one thing he has that wish I had, and that is tremendous confidence. He is one of the few bassists who can do an entire record by themselves and sound good.

JB: *Well, this outside the realm of jazz guitar, but you have done some solo guitar recordings of major orchestral works of Gershwin and Stravinsky.*
LC: Yeah, I still do a few of the easier things, but that music is so hard, and I memorize it to perform it. Otherwise, if I was just recording, it I would read it. Frankly, I am disappointed we didn't get a little more response than we have had to those recordings.

JB: *Was it the challenge that motivated you to do those?*
LC: The challenge was very good for me to do those, but if I had it to do over again, I would use a different guitar for the Stravinsky. I really used the wrong guitar and we did it in too much of a hurry; we did three ballets of Stravinsky in two days. I think we should have done it with more care. If we had, we might have had a masterpiece. There is nothing I can do about it now. I tried to go back and relearn the "Firebird" and I got half way through the first movement, and I thought, this stuff is so hard. So many times I would come up against what was written and I would think, I really didn't play that right.

JB: *How long did it take you to learn something like the "Firebird?"*
LC: I got it down fairly quickly; it was the *Rite of Spring* that was the b-i-t-c-h. I would practice 8-10 hours a day. My fingers felt like they were falling apart. They cramped up. I couldn't believe it. All I can say is that it really prepared me for the concertos that I have written for guitar and orchestra.

JB: *How many concertos have you written?*
LC: I have written two. One for two guitars and orchestra, and one for solo guitar and orchestra. There is a third one that was commissioned for somebody else and he never played it, and I don't know what to do. You know, I can always write. It is a privilege that I have the talent and the ability to write music.

JB: *How has your playing changed over the years?*
LC: It's simpler, and more musical, more graceful, and the phrasing is smoother. I hope! Then again, I don't know. I only hear mistakes when I listen to my own playing. I can only be objective when I listen to a session a year or so after I did it, when I don't remember the session or the music at all, and it sounds like I am listening to someone else

playing. I am working on my sound, trying to play more like Stan Getz.

JB: *What kind of sound are you looking for?*
LC: Playing with my thumb, to get that deeper sound, but you can't play as many notes.

JB: *Separate from your own playing, where do you see jazz guitar going in the future?*
LC: I think that it is really going to stay in the middle of the mainstream and you are going to get more and more players getting deeper into the mainstream; playing over changes, playing stuff that sounds like jazz that has been around a little bit. You will see players who are really trained, trying to do things a little differently. They may absorb things from other cultures ...Middle Eastern or Far Eastern cultures. I think there will be more use of the guitar synthesizer and there will be more use of double-neck stuff. You will see younger players playing jazz but using whammy bars, solid body guitars, still trying to evoke the emotional depth and artistic depth of jazz but still trying to put their individual voice to it.

JB: *Do you feel that fusion jazz guitar or smooth-jazz guitar has been pretty well exhausted?*
LC: Smooth-jazz as I have experienced it has to be really bland to be accessible. The only players that can play really well and still be heard on those stations are George Benson and Pat Metheny, but all the rest of those players just play a bunch of junk. A few years ago when I was trying to get on those stations, I had to totally simplify my playing, so much that it could have been anybody playing the guitar.

JB: *I remember hearing one of your smooth-jazz albums that was produced by Chuck Loeb.*
LC: Yeah, I had to really hold back on the album.

JB: *You were playing very simply.*
LC: But that album got tremendous airplay. It was the *Fallen Angel* album where I do the digital duet with Wes Montgomery, and that album still gets tremendous airplay.

JB: *I want to move to some of your disciplines on the guitar. Tell me how you practice. I know that you do so much playing that maybe all your practice is on the bandstand?*
LC: When I get ready for a gig I do as many scales as I can, go through as many exercises as I can.

JB: *What are some of the exercises that you do?*
LC: Well, just variations on the scales, doing diminished and whole-tone scales in all the positions.

JB: *So you work a lot on the fundamentals?*
LC: Well, I just play, play, play, all the scales, and maybe some extended harmony arpeggios and some snippets of some tunes, and passages that I find challenging. Sometimes I'll just play a tune like *Giant Steps* for a long time. This puts me in a good place, because everything after that is easy.

JB: *Is there a certain amount of time that you practice each day, or does it vary as you feel you need to practice?*
LC: Well, I didn't touch the guitar for a month until today and got away with it, I guess. But before I go out before a large audience, I will do a lot of practicing plus all the rehearsing that I will do with the band. The more you practice, the less you have to worry that when you are in front of a large audience that you won't be able to play the idea that you hear in your mind. You can focus on just being musical.

JB: *Tell me about the guitar you use.*
LC: This is a new Cort guitar designed by Steve Grimes with an oval hole, which will be called the LCS-2. It has an acoustic pickup in the bridge and the regular Humbuckers, and what I do is combine the two pickups to get a more unusual sound than the archtops that I have used. I have a Cort LCS-1 that is like a big box archtop guitar.

JB: *How did you come about your association with Cort Guitars?*
LC: They found me. There was a club owner in New York and I played a standing-room-only gig at his club that we were all very pleased with. He later lost the club and moved to Chicago and met a gal who was the daughter of the boss of the corporation that makes Cort Guitars. A few years later I was in his area doing a gig and he approached me about doing a signature model for Cort, and I said fine.

JB: *What are some other guitars that you own and occasionally use?*
LC: I have this Super 400 that currently needs some work done on it, and I am hesitant about getting the work done on it because I am afraid that once it gets up to snuff, I will not want to play anything else. I also have a pretty good ES-175, but one of my sons borrowed it. I also have a pretty good Les Paul, you know--- the Mary Ford model, and my other son borrowed that.

JB: *What about your acoustic guitars?*
LC: I have one Ramirez guitar that I play occasionally. I had Steve Grimes make me a big box with an oval hole, like a Django Reinhardt guitar, that I like a lot.

JB: *What kind of amplifier do you use?*
LC: I have an old Fender Twin that I like very much. I also have some amps from Saint Louis Music, Ampegs that are quite good. They are kind of like RJC120s (Roland Jazz Chorus). At the gig tomorrow you will hear me run one pickup through the RJC120 and the other through a Twin Reverb. It is a very interesting sound.

JB: *Do you have these amps customized in any way?*
LC: No. If you know how to play the instrument and take time with your amp, tweaking it, you can get a really nice sound.

JB: *What kind of strings do you use?*
LC: A set that LaBella has made up for me. They are not flat wound; flat wound is too dull sounding.

JB: *What effects do you use?*
LC: I used all of them in my younger years, but now I want a pure straight-ahead sound. Occasionally I'll use a little chorus.

JB: *What is your favorite performance ensemble?*
LC: I like a quartet, either piano, bass and drums with me, or horn, bass and drums. Sometimes vibes, bass and drums. My absolute favorite is piano… doubling on vibes, sax, trumpet, bass and drums, but it is totally impractical, because one can't usually afford to go out with more than a quartet.

JB: *What recording projects do you have coming up?*
LC: The reunion with Steve Marcus. We will be doing that in December of 2001. At this point Steve wants it to be covers of some Pearl Jam, Police and other tunes.

JB: *Modern songs, what may be called future standards?*
LC: I don't really like playing those songs. I've been doing some writing again, I have a piece called *Rhapsody and Blues* based on Gershwin, and I hope to sneak in some of which direction I think this project should go. I also want to do as many sax and guitar duets as I can. I think that is where Steve and I sound the strongest, when just the two of us play together.

JB: *Looking further ahead, what are some projects that you would like to do on the guitar?*
LC: I would like to do some Ravel transcriptions and adapt them to the guitar. I would like to do *Five Easy Pieces* by Stravinsky for guitar and some of the Bartok violin duets for guitar.

JB: *Pretty much exploring classical literature on the guitar?*
LC: Yeah, and I also want to continue writing for the guitar. I love composing. It is an honor to compose. You've got to keep writing, I don't always hit a winner, but you've got to keep trying.

JB: *What advice would you give to a young jazz guitarist?*
LC: Learn to read music well. Discipline yourself to think chords and harmony, not just single lines, but that is really hard to do. Don't listen to just guitar players; try to listen to pianists like Bill Evans, Chick Corea, Kenny Kirkland, and others. Listen to tenor players, and trumpet players. Work on your time and expressing feeling in your playing. Listen to a lot of classical music, even John Williams; his movie scores are very good. Listen to great works of Leonard Bernstein, Aaron Copland, and people like that.

JB: *Well, Larry, thank you very much.*
LC: It has been my pleasure.

*Interview courtesy of Just Jazz Guitar (PO Box 76053, Atlanta, GA 30358)*

# C Scale Exercise with Variations

C Scale

◼ = downstroke,  ∨ = upstroke

First Variation

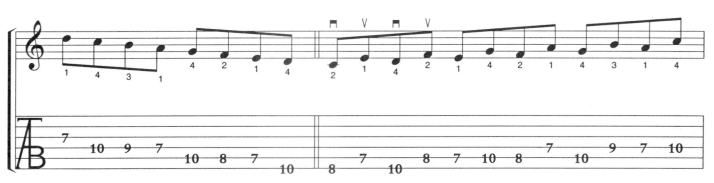

*4th fngr.
short bar*

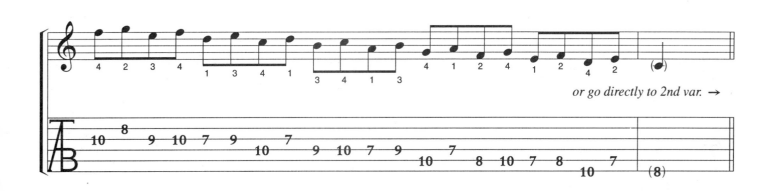

*or go directly to 2nd var.* →

## Second Variation

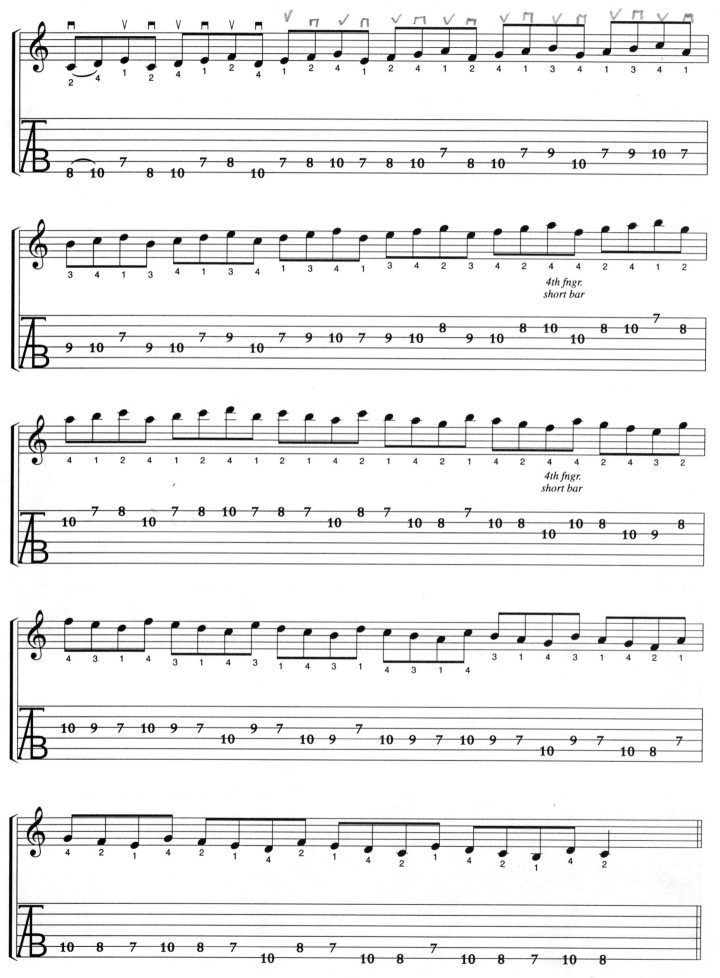

## C Major 7th Positions

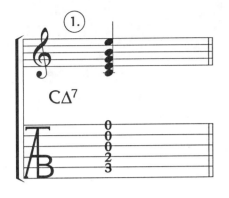 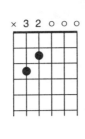

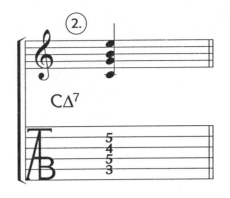 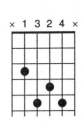

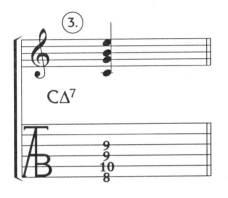 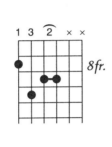

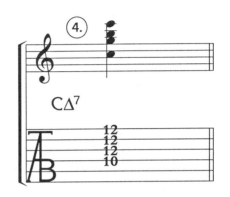 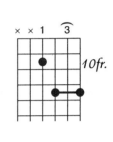

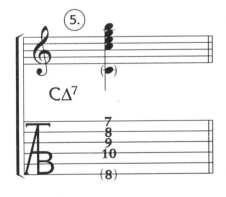 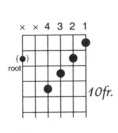

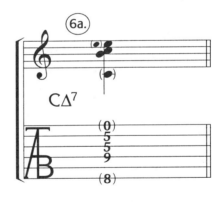 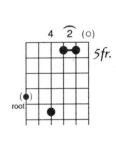

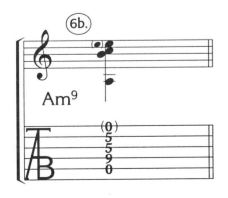 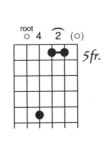

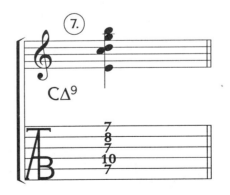 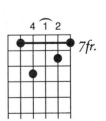

## Explanation of Intervals

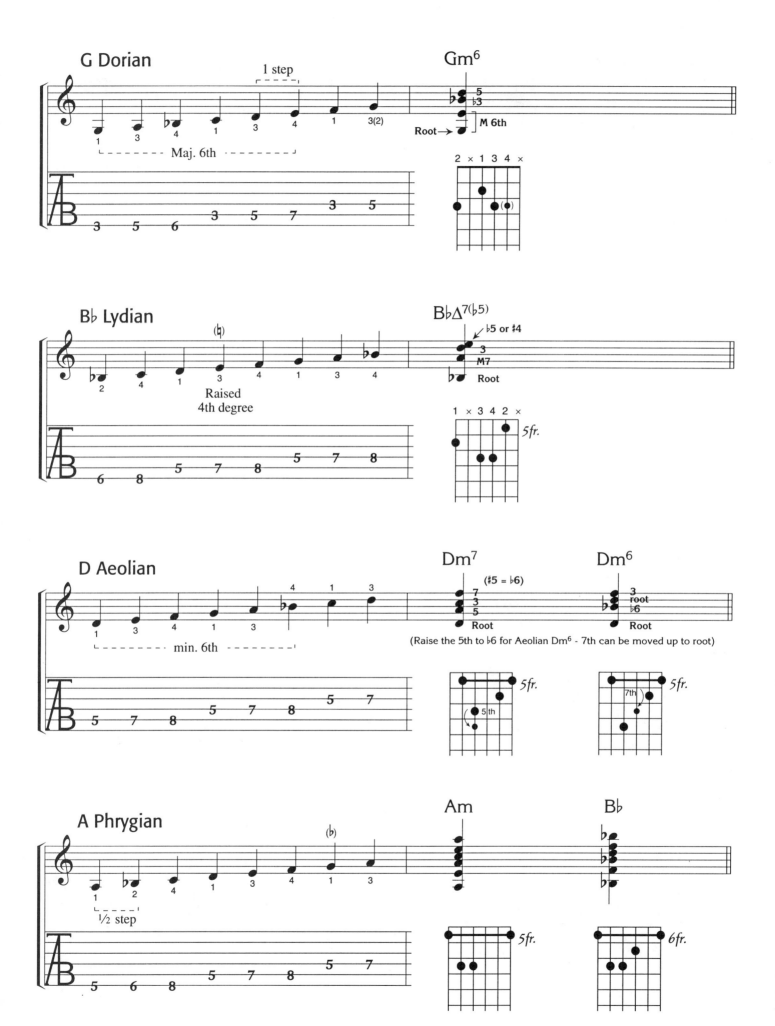

11

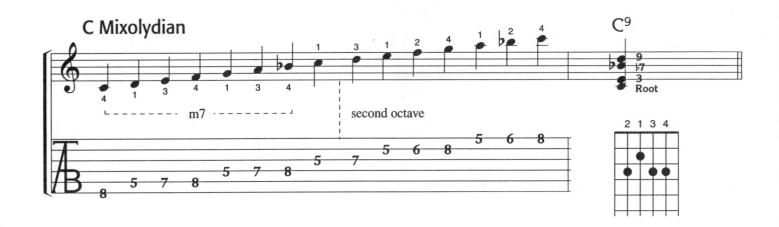

**C Mixolydian**

**E Locrian**

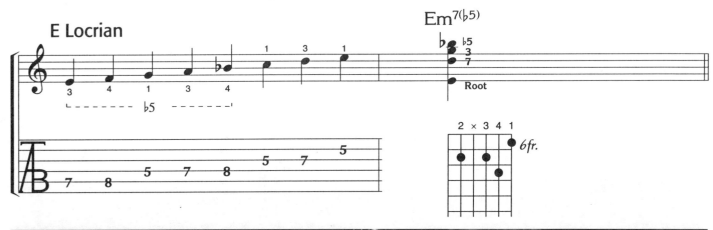

# ARTIFICIAL AND NATURAL HARMONICS

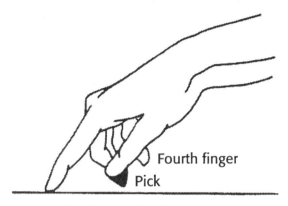

Fourth finger

Pick

Touch string twelve frets
above fretted note for octave.

Cm⁷  C⁹  C⁶/⁹  G¹³  D♭⁶/⁹ (♭5)

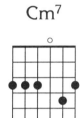 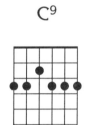 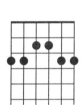  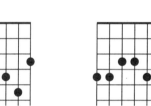

Em⁹ˢᵘˢ⁴  G¹³ˢᵘˢ⁴  GΔ⁷,¹³(♭5)  GΔ⁷

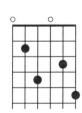  

# 2-4-1-4 EXERCISE

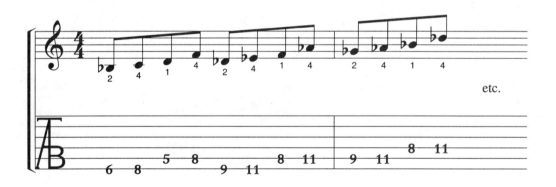

etc.

# Walking Bass Blues

Rob MacKillop

# Mean Kate's Blues

*for Kate Birrell*

Rob MacKillop

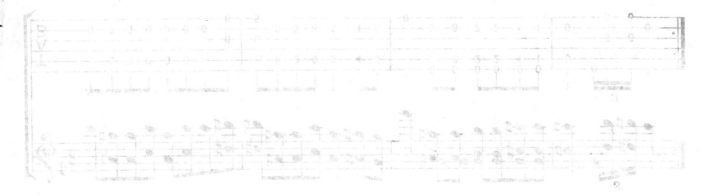

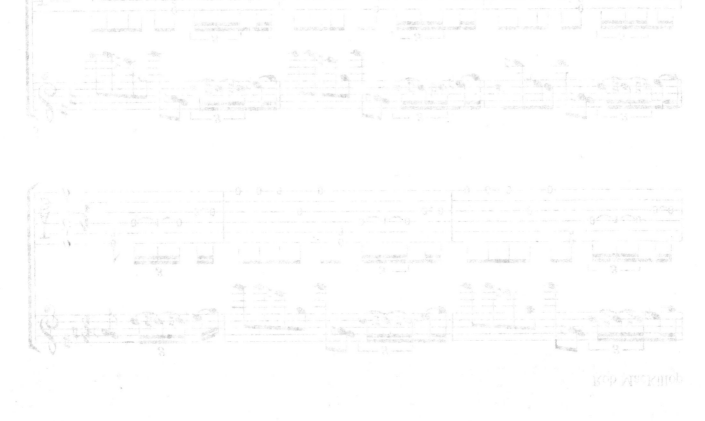

# Japanese Gratitude Exercise

# 7/4 Diminished Exercise

Descending in Whole Steps

etc.

# MINOR THIRDS

# 1+2 SCALES

**Starting on B**

etc.

## 1+2 Exercise A

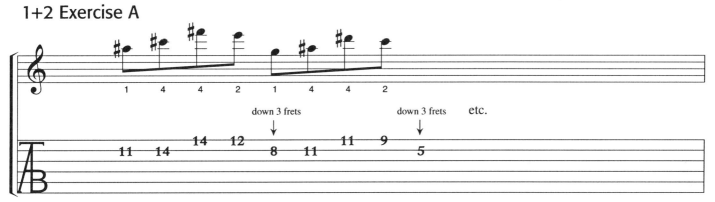

down 3 frets

down 3 frets    etc.

## 1+2 Exercise B

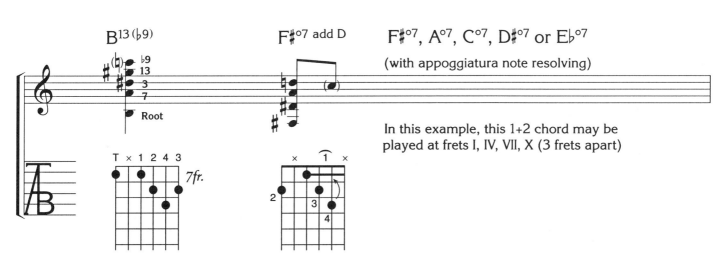

B¹³⁽♭⁹⁾          F♯°⁷ add D          F♯°⁷, A°⁷, C°⁷, D♯°⁷ or E♭°⁷

(with appoggiatura note resolving)

In this example, this 1+2 chord may be
played at frets I, IV, VII, X (3 frets apart)

# 1+2 BLUES

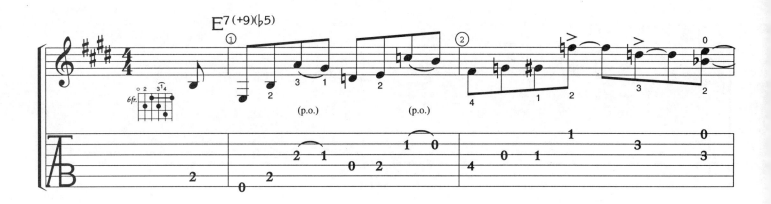

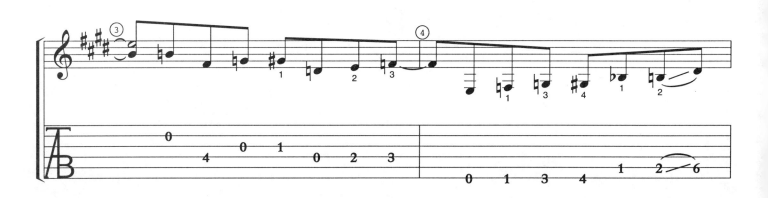

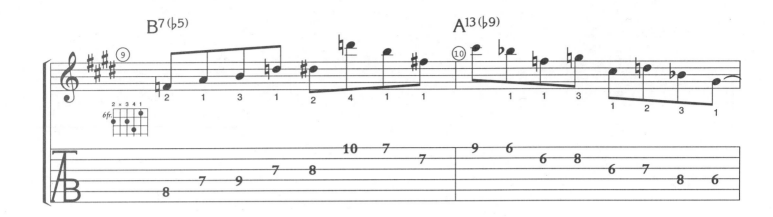

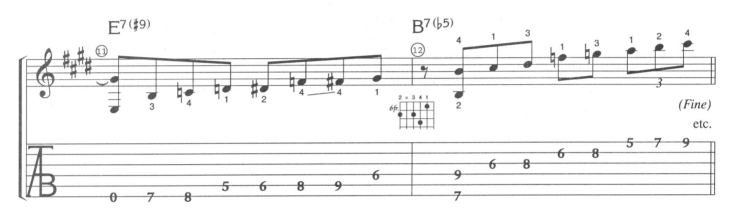

# 1+2 Blues

GUITAR SOLO

A⁷alt.

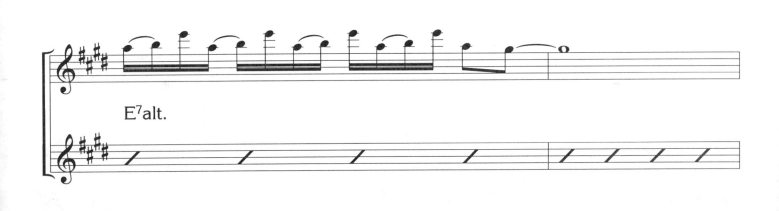

E⁷alt.

B⁷⁽♭⁵⁾          A⁷⁽♭⁵⁾

G♯⁷          G⁷          F♯⁷          F⁷alt.    *D.C. al Fine*

# CD Track Listings

*The audio lessons in this series were originally recorded in the 1970s. They were initially released on audio cassettes. We have gone back to our master tapes to get the best possible sound for this new CD edition. The complete contents of the original recordings have been maintained but certain references to albums that are no longer available or information that is out of date have been edited out. These lessons originally came with different print material. These were handwritten and in some cases offered only tab transcriptions. The lessons have now been typeset in tab/music. As a result some spoken references on the CDs regarding page numbers or a position of a line or phrase on a page may differ slightly from the written tab/music in this new edition. We have annotated as carefully and exactly as possible what each track on the CDs present. Please use these track descriptions as your reference guide.*

## Lesson One

Track 1: Introduction
Track 2: Tuning
Track 3: Teaching of C Scale
Track 4: Plays slowly C Scale
Track 5: Teaching of First Variation of C Scale
Track 6: Teaching of Second Variation ascending of C Scale
Track 7: Plays slowly Second Variation ascending of C Scale
Track 8: Teaching of Second Variation descending of C Scale
Track 9: Plays slowly C Scale and first and second variations of C Scale
Track 10: Plays slightly faster C Scale and first and second variations of C Scale
Track 11: Plays up to tempo C Scale and first and second variations of C Scale
Track 12: Closing thoughts and discussion of playing exercises in Eb
Track 13: Plays up to tempo exercises in Eb
Track 14: Teaching of chord voicings of C Major 7th - chord #1
Track 15: Teaching of chord voicings of C Major 7th - chord #2
Track 16: Teaching of chord voicings of C Major 7th - chord #3
Track 17: Teaching of chord voicings of C Major 7th - chord #4
Track 18: Teaching of chord voicings of C Major 7th - chord #5

Track 19: Teaching of chord voicings of C Major 7th - chord #6
Track 20: Teaching of chord voicings of C Major 7th - chord #7
Track 21: Discussion of Modes
Track 22: Teaching of another C Major 7th
Track 23: Discussion of relationship of chords to modes
Track 24: Discussion of Dorian Mode
Track 25: Discussion of Phrygian Mode
Track 26: Discussion of Lydian Mode
Track 27: Discussion of Mixolydian Mode
Track 28: Discussion of Aeolian Mode
Track 29: Discussion of Locrian Mode
Track 30: Discussion of transposing modes
Track 31: Discussion of Lydian Mode in Bb
Track 32: Discussion of Aeolian Mode in D
Track 33: Discussion of Phrygian Mode in A
Track 34: Discussion of Mixolydian Mode in C
Track 35: Discussion of Locrian Mode in E and closing thoughts

## Lesson Two

Track 1: Introduction
Track 2: Demonstration of artificial and natural harmonics
Track 3: Tuning
Track 4: Teaching of the Ripple Technique and artificial harmonics
Track 5: Teaching of Ripple Technique using both hands
Track 6: Plays slowly Ripple effect
Track 7: Teaching of an alternate Ripple effect
Track 8: Plays chromatic ascending harmonics
Track 9: Plays chromatic ascending harmonics a little faster
Track 10: Teaching of additional techniques for playing artificial harmonics
Track 11: Teaching of Ripple effect against barred position
Track 12: Descending and ascending Ripple effect
Track 13: Further discussion of grand bar and the Cmin7sus4
Track 14: Playing of Cm7sus4
Track 15: Teaching of C9
Track 16: Playing of C9
Track 17: Teaching C6/9
Track 18: Playing of C6/9

Track 19: Teaching of G13
Track 20: Playing of G13
Track 21: Teaching Db6/9(b5)
Track 22: Playing of Db6/9(b5)
Track 23: Teaching of Em9sus4
Track 24: Teaching of G13sus4
Track 25: Teaching of 2-4-1-4 Exercise
Track 26: Plays slowly 2-4-1-4 Exercise
Track 27: Plays faster 2-4-1-4 Exercise
Track 28: Teaching of Japanese Gratitude Exercise
Track 29: Plays slowly Japanese Gratitude Exercise
Track 30: Plays Japanese Gratitude Exercise taking down in whole steps
Track 31: Plays faster Japanese Gratitude Exercise taking down in whole steps
Track 32: Teaching of 7/4 Diminished Exercise descending in whole steps
Track 33: Plays slowly 7/4 Diminished Exercise descending in whole steps
Track 34: Plays faster 7/4 Diminished Exercise descending in whole steps
Track 35: Closing thoughts

## Lesson Three

Track 1: Introduction
Track 2: Tuning
Track 3: Teaching of exercises in Minor Thirds
Track 4: Plays slowly first four bars of exercise in Minor Thirds
Track 5: Teaching of exercise in Minor Thirds going up in half steps
Track 6: Teaching of second exercise in Minor Thirds going up in half steps
Track 7: Closing discussion of exercise in Minor Thirds
Track 8: Teaching of 1+2 Scale
Track 9: Plays slowly ascending 1+2 Scale
Track 10: Teaching of descending 1+2 Scale
Track 11: Plays slowly 1+2 Scale ascending and descending
Track 12: Plays faster 1+2 Scale ascending and descending
Track 13: Teaching of variation to 1+2 Scale

Track 14: Plays slowly variation to 1+2 Scale
Track 15: Teaching of second variation to 1+2 Scale
Track 16: Plays second variation to 1+2 Scale
Track 17: Teaching of B 1+2 Scale with B13b9 chord
Track 18: Larry performs 1+2 Blues
Track 19: Teaching of first four bars of 1+2 Blues
Track 20: Plays slowly first four bars of 1+2 Blues
Track 21: Teaching from fifth bar to end of 1+2 Blues
Track 22: Plays 1+2 Blues at medium tempo
Track 23: Plays 1+2 Blues at slow tempo
Track 24: Teaching of chords to 1+2 Blues
Track 25: Larry plays chord backup for student to solo over
Track 26: Closing thoughts